PETRELLA, THE GILLIAN PRINCESS

By

Chiara Talluto

A & S
MERCURY
EYES
PUBLISHING

Parents/Guardians/Fairy Tale Enthusiasts

Thank you for purchasing *Petrella, the Gillian Princess*. This unique fairy tale interweaves themes similar to *The Little Mermaid, Cinderella, Tangled, Sleeping Beauty*, and *Noah's Ark*. It's a story of hope, bravery, and triumph.

My hope is that you will read it with your child, or they can read it to themselves.

Dedication

To my daughters.

May you always look at this world by its potential, and not by its demise.

Never be afraid to pursue your dreams and follow your heart.

Stand up and stand firm for God;

Be strong in your faith;

Be true to yourself;

Believe in the magic of love.

You are worthy, and you are worth it.

Make every moment of your life matter.

Make a difference.

Risk it all for the right cause.

Part I: Deceptive Renewal

Calendar Year: 2041 A.D.

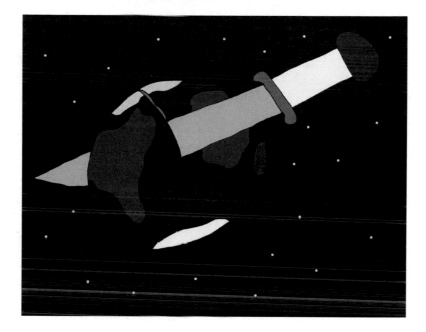

The Destruction of Earth.

Earth was in a perilous state. There was idolatry, greed, and apathy among the humans. God was angry with the world.

Thousands of years earlier, He brought the flood, and promised never again to bring another flood to the land, nor destroy all the living creatures. But, many, many years passed, and things on Earth had worsened once again. God warned the humans to change their evil ways, but no one

1

heeded his command.

And so, on a sunny Friday afternoon, a large silver sword with an ivory handle cut through the clouds and sliced the Earth in half. The skies darkened and it had become night; all the water shifted and drained from the land. There were quakes, landslides, volcanic eruptions; many animals and humans perished. It took years, many years, to rebuild the world.

The Earth was no more and Yemell evolved. In this new world, there were two forms of life: those that lived on land, the surviving humans and animals; and those that lived in the water, creatures of the sea and a new species, the Gillians. They had human-like heads and torsos, fish-like tails, and could breathe through their noses as well as gills located on the sides of their ribs.

Yemell's Underwater Kingdoms.

God was very pleased with his new creation. More than anything, He wanted the Humans and Gillians to love each other and live harmoniously. However, neither species cared for one another because secretly they each wanted to be the superior species on Yemell.

Land and water kingdoms arose; governments were established, and covenants and laws were enacted to help maintain order. Together, the Gillians and the Humans just coexisted on Yemell, as man and animals had done before

3

on Earth.

God reluctantly accepted their plan of coexistence; one without interaction, and without love for one another. And so, He gave the Humans and Gillians *Five Rules* they had to adhere to in order to live freely on Yemell:

God's Five Rules.

He made it clear that if *any* of these rules were not followed, great hatred and animosity would follow, eventually resulting in Yemell's self-destruction.

4

The Mighty King Hermas.

KING HERMAS WAS THE KING of the Anglon Kingdom. He had reigned for many, many years. He was a very handsome Gillian, sporting long bronze-colored hair and a white flowing beard which reached the middle of his chest. He was thick and muscular.

A fearless soldier under the leadership of King Caputa, his mentor, Hermas had helped him conquer the Atlantic and Pacific Kingdoms. He then worked tirelessly up through the ranks of the Anglon Kingdom. When King

Caputa died, Hermas took his place. Three decades had passed under Hermas' powerful hand. His position, he believed, was as almighty as God himself.

The King's plan had been to train his eldest and only son, Raja, to replace him when the time was right. However, a terrible accident involving his beloved wife, Azel, tragically took both of their lives three years earlier. This was a loss Hermas could not grapple with. His only other heir was his precious eighteen-year-old daughter, Princess Petrella.

Petrella was a young, beautiful Gillian princess with long, silky, golden hair; her eyes were the color of brown pearls. Lean and strong, she often glided across the ocean floor alone, playing with orcas, dolphins, flounder, and other sea creatures. According to Gillian law, princesses could not rule kingdoms. They were required to marry a wealthier prince from another kingdom.

The Gentle Queen Azel.

PETRELLA MISSED HER MOTHER very much. Queen Azel had been a beautiful queen with curly, copper hair, and pink skin. She was a gentle soul, exceedingly loving toward her and Raja, and faithful and patient toward their father.

An educator at heart, Azel spent many evenings teaching them *The Volumb*, a sacred book written by Gillian scholars, primarily about their history, their purpose, and instructions for living purely on Yemell, along with God's

Five Rules.

A natural storyteller, the queen shared many fables with her children once told to her by her mother about love and perseverance.

Petrella adored stories about love the most. One particular favorite that Azel recounted was a Gillian story about Queen Bethsheeba and Medith. Medith had been a long-time servant to the Queen and her husband, King Samul. Medith was very short, compared to the average-sized male Gillian. He was born without his right arm, and his face was deformed. Despite his physical abnormalities, he was exceedingly loyal and kind, especially toward the Queen. Many made fun of him and abused him, including the King, but Bethsheeba felt sympathetic toward her servant. An innocent friendship developed; eventually the two fell in love.

When King Samul found out about their relationship, he banished his wife and Medith from the kingdom. The King was so enraged by what had transpired that he sent messengers to all the surrounding kingdoms, warning other kings of their recent trespasses, and demanding they not allow Bethsheeba and Medith entrance through their gates.

As the story goes, somehow the two lovers found a place to live, far, far away in the sea. No one knows where for certain. They had two offspring: one female and one male. Both had some kind of deformity. The descendants of that relationship are black with straight, maroon-colored hair. They are believed to be the most loving and peaceful of all Gillians. But because of their history, they have been cast out from most of the sea world.

Petrella relished the story so much because even though Bethsheeba and Medith were different, they made their relationship work through their honest love for one another, and they stayed bonded, while evil tried breaking them apart. Love had prevailed over evil.

Queen Azel would often encourage her daughter, "Be

that girl: like Bethsheeba. Find the good in others, and always be true to yourself. Follow God's *Five Rules* and the teachings of the *Volumb*. One day, you will be rewarded for your obedience."

Petrella appreciated everything that her mother had taught her. She did her best every day in her studies, listened to her parents, and dreamed of falling in love with the right Gillian and living happily ever after.

The Beautiful Princess Petrella.

PRINCESS PETRELLA WAS ONE of the most sought-after females in the sea. At least once a month, suitors from kingdoms far and wide converged in Anglon's Palace Great Hall, asking King Hermas' permission for Petrella's hand, but his daughter expressed no interest in any of them, claiming they weren't the right ones. The King was frustrated, and thus, took it upon himself to find the *perfect* Gillian male to succeed him, to assure the prosperity of the Anglon Kingdom, and persuade his daughter to become the best queen he knew she could be.

With this goal in mind, Hermas sought out King Kahel from the Jesuit Kingdom. Kahel had a son, Prince Batavia. A brown-skinned male of twenty-six, he was a warrior, possessing natural "fighter" characteristics, something that Hermas' son Raja never had.

Time was not on King Hermas' side. His support was waning. He ruled his lower and middle-class Gillians with intimidation and fear, while keeping the elite fat and

11

greedy. There were also rumors of a rebel militia gaining power, the *Zioppa*, a group of younger anti-government Gillians. Already, this group had overtaken several kingdoms, and Hermas was fearful of any retaliation against him. In order to protect himself and his empire, he realized that he must align with a stronger kingdom and inaugurate a new king as soon as possible.

Hermas knew he could lose his kingdom if it wasn't strengthened in time, and more importantly, his health was beginning to deteriorate. In order to expedite matters and bring the young Gillians together, he organized a gala. King Hermas told his daughter that the purpose of this celebration was to invite King Kahel to their kingdom because they had recently become friends.

But unbeknownst to Petrella, it was all part of her father's *grand* plan, an attempt to form a strategic alliance, to partner with King Kahel and his son so that the Anglon Kingdom would continue to thrive, eliminating the possibility of being overthrown by the *Zioppa* rebels. There was a catch. In order for the alliance to work, she'd have no choice but to marry Batavia. Desperation and pressure weighed on King Hermas' psyche. He hoped he could convince Petrella to be with Batavia.

Petrella was unaware of the twist of fate that lay before her. However, coming from royalty, she was accustomed to grand festivities because her parents entertained a lot. Her father promised her an orchestra, and she was looking forward to hearing songs played on instruments crafted out of sea shells and rock.

Listening to music was what Petrella enjoyed the most besides exploring the ocean. In the afternoons, after school, she would swim to Metalicah Pointe, a tidal island that was connected to the mainland. There, she'd spend hours bobbing in the waves, listening to music wafting through the air and watching the beautiful humans basking in the hot sun at the RavenZedd Compound.

The Glorious RavenZedd Compound.

A grand structure, the compound was fifteen stories high. She had heard the entrance and the rooms were decorated in gold and white lace, and the bathrooms were so large that six humans could bathe together comfortably in tubs filled with rich oils and perfumes. The wealthiest humans frequented the establishment, gallivanting in the clear water and on the meticulously combed beach.

PETRELLA HAD BEEN COMING to Metalicah Pointe for quite some time. The small island was not inhabited, but it did have a church. Its colorful stained glass windows were broken and structurally, the building was not safe.

At one time, the church was a place of prayer and spiritual refuge; at least that's what her mother had told her. It was now long abandoned, but the island with the church was a good distance away from the mainland, and she used it as a cover to observe the humans without being discovered.

During her adventures to Metalicah Pointe, Petrella became particularly enchanted with watching one human male at the RavenZedd Compound. The male folded beach chairs and cleaned tables. Gifted with mahogany, wavy hair, and pale skin, she noticed that he was always gracious to his patrons and smiled often. There was something common and kind about him that drew her to him and it gave her goosebumps.

Her father forbade Petrella from going to Metalicah Pointe and watching the humans. By an instituted covenant, Gillians and Humans were not allowed to seek relations with one another. Hermas often had one of his palace guards, Amos, keep watch over his daughter. However, Petrella knew the sea very well and was a fast swimmer; she made sure he lost her trail every time. This continuous defiance infuriated the King; he wished more than anything to hasten the betrothal of his daughter to Batavia.

One day, when Petrella arrived at Metalicah Pointe, she ogled five humans standing in a semicircle playing with strange-looking instruments at the RavenZedd Compound.

Pleasing sounds filled the air and Petrella hummed to the beat, longing to join the humans as they danced about. Even though the sea had its beauty, she felt like a prisoner within her own kingdom. She was lonely, often missing her mother and brother, while yearning for this thing called "love". *If Bethsheeba and Medith found love, might I too?*

Suddenly, Petrella spotted the smiling young human, the one she'd been watching. He was dancing with a female. He twirled the woman in his arms, laughing and giggling. Petrella swam closer toward the compound; close enough for him to notice her. The man turned, stopped, and waved.

Their eyes locked in an electrifying trance. Her heart skipped a beat. She couldn't break his gaze. Finally, Petrella shook her head, frightened of this feeling shooting through her body. Without another thought, she dipped and disappeared into the water.

Finerd, the Smiling Human.

On a few other occasions, she felt the same way after spying the young man at the RavenZedd Compound. *Why am I experiencing this exhilaration within my heart?* She hadn't any answers; she was awfully confused.

THE EVENING OF THE GALA had arrived; it was to be held in the Palace square. Lush gardens, fragrant flowers and glowing starfish illuminated the festive ambiance. Extended family and specially invited royal ambassadors from other kingdoms completed the glorious ensemble.

Dressed in glittering jewelry and a gold and ruby eye mask,

Petrella stood by her father while King Kahel, his wife,

Queen Deijing, and their son, Prince Batavia, greeted them.

Prince Batavia, the Strong Warrior.

Batavia stood tall, sporting a gold and silver crown

sitting upon his raven-colored hair. His brown muscles

bulged in his leather warrior attire. He and King Hermas

embraced, slapping each other on their backs. They began

talking about war and the advantages of a strong

government, both topics bored Petrella. She began whistling a tune that she had heard at Metalicah Pointe earlier that afternoon.

King Hermas cleared his throat. "My dear, Petrella, I give you..." he caught himself, "I mean, this is King Kahel's son, Prince Batavia."

Petrella curtsied and extended her hand to Batavia as she was groomed to do with all elite families. From the corner of her eye, she caught her father and Batavia nodding to each other. Instantly, she suspected he had ulterior motives.

Retracting her hand and turning toward the King, she asked, "What's going on?"

All three Gillian males shrugged their shoulders.

"What do you mean?" The King scrunched his face.

Flexing his forearm, Batavia gave her a seductive wink.

Petrella gasped and pointed, "Do you expect that him and I should...?" She was so taken aback that she lost her voice.

In the last few days leading up to the gala, Petrella had overheard whispers about King Kahel and his family in the square. The King was known to be brutal, often slaughtering Gillians that refused to follow his laws. His son, Batavia, was a "Gillianizer," a harasser and assaulter of females. He wasn't well-liked and was considered crude, rude, and brash. She had been disgusted and tried speaking to her father about the rumors, but he had dismissed her without comment.

Gathering her wits about her, Petrella grabbed her father's arm, saying, "May we speak alone, please?"

"Honey, now, you listen to me," Hermas rationalized, "we could—"

"...Father?"

Hermas nodded, embarrassed, "Could you excuse us for one moment?"

King Kahel and his family moved aside.

Now with his full attention, Petrella asked, "Is this why

Chiara Talluto

you planned the gala? So you could arrange that I should marry that Gillian! Why didn't you consult with me first?"

The King stroked his beard and glared at his daughter. "The choices are limited. Besides, every Gillian male that has asked for your hand, you've dismissed. I had to do something."

She took a breath and lowered her voice. "I know your health has not been good and you have no heir to your kingdom, but I refuse to have anything to do with Batavia. King Kahel and his family are not decent Gillians. I've heard how they treat their own."

King Hermas grabbed her by the shoulders. "We are in dire straits; rebels will take over Anglon if I do nothing."

"Father, please, you're hurting me."

He tightened his grip. "I have reigned over this kingdom for thirty plus years. Your brother is dead, and frankly, he wouldn't have been strong enough to handle this kingdom anyway. He was too soft, just like your mother. But, *I* was

22

willing to give him the chance to rule. I have to look after what I have worked hard to build. If this means aligning with King Kahel and his son, to keep this kingdom from falling, so be it."

Hermas pulled at her harder. "I've looked upon and studied many Gillian princes. This is the one I want to rule Anglon after I am gone."

Tears fell down Petrella's face as she pulled away from his grasp. "What about me? I want to fall in love, Father. Just like you and Mother. And now, you're taking that opportunity away from me."

King Hermas adjusted his posture, "It's been decided; you will marry Batavia."

Petrella sniffled, remembering when her father was a loving Gillian and actually paid attention to her. Oh, how she missed the days when they'd play in the garden where she pretended to be a bride, and he would play her prince. Her mother, Queen Azel, had helped tame him while she was alive; he had been compassionate toward *all* the Gillians in his kingdom for a time. But since her mother and brother's passing, King Hermas had changed; he was consumed, constantly trying to strengthen his kingdom.

Shaking her head, Petrella demanded. "What's happened to you? I miss the father you used to be. *You* are not the same, but *I* am still that girl—your faithful daughter."

The King turned away from her and growled.

"Mother would be disappointed." She pushed past her father and swam away in desperation.

Hermas drew a fist at her fleeting form. "I am King here, and I will do what I want."

Batavia went up to him. "Don't worry, sir. I'll get her. I'll fix everything."

Rushing through flowing seaweed, past hundreds of jellyfish, schools of sardines, sea ravens, octopi, and barracudas, Petrella swam fast. She went through a sunken ship and saw Batavia attempting to catch up to her.

He came up from behind, near a Staghorn coral reef, and bear-hugged her.

"You heard what your Father said, you are mine!" His foul breath assaulted her senses.

Twisting around, Petrella slapped his face.

"Ha." Batavia extended his neck and puffed out his chest. "We *are* getting married, and then I will be ruler of *Anglon* and leader of *Zioppa*."

Oh, no! He is part of the Zioppa militia, the rebels destroying other kingdoms. She tried clawing at his eyes, but Batavia grabbed the young woman in a tight grip and pushed her into the coral. Her eyes welled as she squirmed and wiggled under his hold, but he was too strong —the coral's cylindrical branches ripped deeply into Petrella's flesh.

"You. Are. Mine!" The warrior snarled.

She winced and cried out in pain. When he freed her, she took the opportunity to strike his face again and punch him in the stomach. As Batavia doubled over, she escaped; her blood trailed behind her.

Petrella raced through the water, breathing hard, removing her jewelry and her mask—letting them fall to the seafloor. *Where can I go to get away from Batavia? I want to swim away from everyone.* Without thinking, she turned and headed for Metalicah Pointe.

Part II: Close Encounter

Petrella surfaced from the water at Metalicah Pointe; coughing and vomiting after what had just happened. It was completely dark. She tried touching the gashes and slashes on her back, but couldn't reach them, nor could she see how deep they were. Her back felt like it was on fire.

Several yards away, just east of the RavenZedd Compound, she sighted a pier. A tall pole with a hanging square lighted lantern provided a silvery sheen over the tranquil water. Sitting cross-legged on the pier was a human male dressed in a brown shirt and dark pants. He was holding his face between his hands and resembled the human she'd been spying at the compound.

Petrella glided toward the structure quietly, fearful of making a sound and being detected, wanting only to get a closer glimpse of him. As she approached, her arm touched something sharp drifting in the water.

"Ouch!" she blurted out.

The male jolted up from his sitting position, "Who's

there?"

He wiped his eyes with the back of his hand and saw her; he stared, mesmerized by her bright elegance. Her face glistened. He had heard and seen Gillian females and had adored their good looks, but this one was gorgeous beyond belief. Her skin was the color of a seashell; her hair was long and yellow.

...My goodness. It's her, the one who has been swimming near the compound!

She continued to float in the water, watching him as he looked at her. He crept closer to the edge of the pier. Crouching down, he motioned with his hand. "It's okay, I won't hurt you. Please come closer."

Petrella, still shivering, hesitated. "Were you crying, just now?"

He pulled his hand back and sat down cross-legged again. "Ah..." His heart ached and he couldn't mask his pain any longer. "My mother died today."

"I'm so sorry," she offered.

He bit at his fingernail, "Me, too."

She kicked up her fin. "What's your name?"

He looked up. "Finerd, what's yours?"

"...Petrella."

Finerd jerked up. "...Petrella? You mean like Princess Petrella of Anglon? I've heard of you."

She nodded, embarrassed.

He fell to his knees. "...Your highness."

Petrella moved away, unsure of what to do. Her back was raw, the water stung her cuts.

Finerd bent forward. "Wait; stop, where are you going?"

She turned back toward him.

"Could you come out of the water and sit with me for a while?"

Petrella faced this young human and thought about it for a moment. She knew what would happen if she stayed out of the water too long—her gills would dry. However, curiosity got the best of her, and she was willing to take the risk. She wanted to sit next to him, to touch his flesh.

Petrella nodded, "Okay, I'll need some help, though; I'm hurt."

"Yes, yes, no problem. Come over here."

Finerd bent down and reached for her hand. She was lighter than he expected. Her body was trim. He lifted her out of the water, settling her down on the pier, carefully adjusting her fin over the edge.

He noticed her exposed flesh. "Whoa..." he stumbled, "you're naked."

Petrella looked down, covering herself with her hair. Suddenly she remembered human females wore clothing. "Please, forgive me."

"No, no...I mean, yes, here, wear this," he removed his shirt and handed it to her. "Put this on."

Petrella stared up at his bare chest. A tattoo of a star encircled his left chest muscle.

She tried putting the shirt on but was in so much pain. "Ah...I can't—"

Finerd glanced at her back. She had several wounds that were long and deep, but there wasn't any bleeding. "I see you're badly injured."

He scanned the pier. Remembering his bag, he pulled out a green cloak. "You'll be okay with this. Let me put it around you."

"Thank you," Petrella whispered as Finerd gingerly draped it over her.

The young man sat down next to her, his long legs dangling over the dock. "What happened to you?"

The trees rustled around them. Her fin waggled in the wind. Petrella quivered under the cloak. She knew she couldn't stay out of the water very long. "I scratched myself on a coral reef."

Finerd nodded, but wasn't convinced. "That doesn't look like coral scratches to me."

Unable to tell Finerd the truth, thinking of anything to distract her mind, Petrella quickly reached over and touched the star on his chest. His skin was warm. "I like it."

Electricity flowed through Finerd's body; her delicate touch had triggered an unexpected reaction and he exhaled slowly. "Thank you..."

Petrella continued to trace the star with her fingers.

Attempting to calm his beating heart, he said, "My mom used to tell me I was born under a shower of stars."

"It's amazing."

Finerd trembled. "You're the girl in the sea."

Petrella smiled, "Yes, it is I."

"I...I haven't been able to stop thinking about you. You are beautiful."

"And, you are just as beautiful."

They sat for a bit, staring out into the night, and then Finerd began asking her questions about life in the water. She told him about her father, King Hermas, what the

Anglon Kingdom was like, and the joy she felt when listening to music. She also told him about losing her mother and brother, and how much she missed them.

"I'm sorry for your loss. Your kingdom still sounds like a great place to live."

Petrella shook her head. She felt privileged being a princess, but she preferred a simpler life, one without guards and servants. "It's not as wonderful as it seems."

Finerd nodded in agreement. "I can say the same thing about living on land. At least you have the sea."

"I can't live on land, but you can."

"True, but we need water for drinking and bathing."

"And I need 'water' to live," she replied with a smirk.

Finerd grinned, lowering his voice, "President Tuskana is a ruthless leader. We slave while he lives in amusing luxury; sitting in his 'White House' proclaiming that everything is okay on the land, but in reality, there is constant fighting and war. There are eyes and ears everywhere; we need to be careful with everything we say and do."

Petrella poked at him. "You have one ruthless leader while we have too many ruthless kings who want to be just like your president."

They laughed nervously at their situations, knowing the consequences if they were ever found together... *Severe punishment to those Humans and Gillians seen talking to each other!*

Finerd stared at the calm water. "The sea seems so tranquil tonight."

Petrella hugged her cloak. "It is, at times. Many Gillians have ruined that tranquility. It is terribly crowded with the building of new kingdoms. I love the colorful sea life, though. There is no judgment or competition, only camaraderie among the sea's creatures."

Finerd put his arm around her, a gesture he found too easy and comfortable with this female—this Gillian princess. "I couldn't agree more."

She squeezed her eyes to try to diffuse the wrenching spasms going through her spine.

He gently turned her face toward him, stroking her hair. "I can't explain it, but I like you. I like you a lot. However, my mind is desperate for the truth. Please tell me what *really* happened to you?"

Princess Petrella and Finerd at the pier.

Petrella folded into his body and clung to his neck. "Oh, you are too kind. Thank you. I like you too."

He touched her face. "Well?"

Sighing, she replied. "I'm supposed to marry a Gillian prince, but he is evil. I just found out he's part of a rebel group taking over and destroying some of our kingdoms. In fact, I swam here because he...he..." she couldn't finish. Petrella began to sob, recalling what he'd done to her.

Through clenched teeth, Finerd blurted. "He hurt you, didn't he?"

She nodded weakly. "I shouldn't have said anything. This lovely moment with you is ruined."

"Why, I'll—"

Petrella shook her head and grabbed his hand. "You can't do anything, Finerd. You're a Human. I have to go to my father and tell him everything," she sniffled. "I'm sorry I told you. I don't even know you that well, yet, I feel like I've known you all my life."

He held her hand tightly. "Crazy isn't it? What's even crazier is that we're both grieving about something."

Petrella sighed again. "Unfortunately, yes. But, do tell me more about you. I feel so happy here with you."

They talked for a while longer. Finerd was nineteen-years-old and worked at the RavenZedd Compound. His mother had been sick and in a special care facility. He was trying to save up enough money for her to see an *Arowdithe*—a human who specialized in natural medicine. While on a lunch break, he heard about his mother's passing; the news completely devastated him. They lived far away and now he had five younger siblings to feed.

"I love sitting here and looking at the water. I came here tonight after work to try and figure out what I should do next before I go home. And then you showed up."

Petrella listened, her heart bursting with empathy. Having observed him for weeks now, she realized how intense her attraction was to him too. *I'm falling for a*

Human. This is very wrong. Even so, I can't help myself. Is this what love feels like? They were still talking when they heard someone calling his name.

Finerd shuffled to his feet, adrenaline pulsed through his body. "You must leave immediately."

She fumbled with the cloak, not wanting this time to end.

Worried for her safety, he said, "Here, give it to me. I want to see you again. I *must* see you. Let's meet here tomorrow night, same time?"

Petrella nodded; slithering off the pier and into the water just as two human males approached Finerd.

Not too far off, Batavia witnessed the entire exchange. *So this is where you've been?* He plunged back into the sea and swam toward King Hermas' Palace. He had to get back there before Petrella.

Part III: Redemption

The gala was over. The square was empty as Petrella approached the door of the Palace. It was flung open and two guards, Amos and Rooper, seized her.

"Let me go. What is going on, Amos? I want to see my Father!" she jerked and squirmed, but to no avail.

"...Father! ...Father!"

King Hermas stood before her, shaking his head. "You ruined our evening. You have disappointed me, my daughter."

"Father, please! Batavia is not who you think he is. He's with the *Zioppa* rebels. Don't go through with this alliance. It's a trick. Do you hear me, my King?"

Amos and Rooper looked at one another and eased their grip. They had heard about Batavia and his treatment of Gillian females, but with this new revelation, fear raced through their bones.

"Nonsense, my child, the Kahel family is not affiliated with those degenerates. I know where you've been, though,

47

sitting with a Human! You will never go to Metalicah Pointe again."

Petrella shuddered. *How does he know?*

Hermas bellowed, "You've disobeyed me and the laws we've established!"

Batavia appeared at the King's side with a big grin on his face. "Shall I take her off your hands for a bit, sir?"

"No, Father, don't let him touch me!"

King Hermas shook his daughter. "Relations with Humans are forbidden." His voice grew louder, "You will be punished! I will not be made a fool."

"Father, believe me, I did nothing wrong." Petrella twisted about. "*He* is the problem. *He* harmed me! Batavia will destroy us. He will destroy—"

"...Blasphemy!" Batavia charged.

The King grabbed Batavia. "Shut up! I will reprimand my daughter, not you. Now, leave us."

"What about the marriage, sir? Is it still set for next

week?"

Hermas nodded, "Yes, now get out of here."

Batavia winked at Petrella and left.

Still in the grips of the guards, Petrella pleaded with her father once again. "Why don't you believe what I'm saying to you? Why don't you care for me anymore? He is poison. I will not marry him."

King Hermas, about to strike her, cowered and began coughing, "Argh…This is your fault, making me ill. Get her out of here. Bind her and take her to the tower."

"No—!" Petrella wailed as she was dragged away.

The Anglon Prison Tower.

THE TOWER WAS BEHIND THE PALACE. It was a tall, round, brown structure as high as the Palace steeple, and it only contained one large prison cell at the very top. To get to the cell one had to swim up through a dark murky tunnel where all sorts of slimy creatures lurked. Petrella knew about the tower. Most of the Gillians who committed crimes were held there until the day they were publicly tortured in the square. Petrella felt like she was going to her own death, soon to be Batavia's partner. She knew, once they were married, that he would eventually kill her and her father.

Amos and Rooper pulled her along and shoved her into the room, padlocking the door behind her. Once inside, she lay on the floor, trying to catch her breath, massaging her arms to restore circulation where the restraints had burned into her skin. She thought about Finerd and how at peace she felt during that brief period they had spent together.

Petrella's mind raced. She had to escape and get to land, get to Finerd. *I'm not going to marry Batavia, not ever!*

That night, she started to develop a plan of action. But one day moved into the next. Petrella counted them by collecting strands of seaweed that streamed in through the one and only porthole complete with steel bars to prevent escape. She could peek out but couldn't see how many guards were keeping watch over the tower.

Several days passed. The only contact Petrella had with

anyone was when Amos or Rooper brought her food once a day. She was beginning to feel weak and delusional from confinement. Her mind played tricks on her; she imagined Finerd swimming at the porthole, trying to save her, and then holding her close to him. She prayed that he had not forgotten her.

AT THE RAVENZEDD COMPOUND, Finerd was working longer and taking on as many odd jobs as he could to provide food for his younger siblings. He was the head of the household now. His father, Rebus, had left the family four years earlier after the birth of his youngest brother, Titus. With his mother's passing, there was no time to grieve. The burden of the family rested upon his shoulders.

Despite the weary days and nights spent laboring, Finerd always went to the same pier at eleven, the one where he and Petrella had originally met. He felt a strong connection to her and couldn't get her out of his head—with every chore, every movement, Petrella consumed his *every* thought. She was different than human females. There was a sweet vulnerability about her. He wished their relationship could come to fruition. But he knew better. Humans and Gillians just coexisted on Yemell. It was the *agreed-upon* covenant. He couldn't live in the water and she couldn't live on land. And yet every night, he waited for her—hoping to see her.

After five nights of waiting, Finerd's hopes diminished; he believed she'd never return. *Perhaps she has married that prince after all.* Dejected, he looked one more time toward the sea, and then turned, lumbering off the pier.

ON THE SIXTH DAY, the tower cell door opened. Amos, Rooper, and King Hermas entered. Petrella lay on the floor. They rushed to her side.

"Petrella! Petrella! Wake up," Hermas wept. He pulled at her hair. "Oh my, what have I done?"

He shook her shoulders but her eyes never opened. He turned toward the guards, "Get her some medicine, now!"

Rooper scrambled out while Amos helped Hermas lift Petrella onto a bench in the room.

King Hermas caressed her face. "I'm so sorry; I had to do this to teach you a lesson. Everything's in place for the big wedding. It will be a beautiful wedding, like the one you and I used to play together when you were young."

When there was no response from Petrella, the King impatiently turned to Amos. "Go and check on Rooper, see what's taking him so long."

Amos scurried away, leaving the door ajar.

Bigger and stronger, Petrella knew her father's strength, but with his depleting health she also knew his weakness— his ailing stomach. With Amos out of the way, she threw a hard jab to his belly. The King fell over and began vomiting.

As she brushed past him, she cried, "I told you, Father,

Batavia is bad news. I will not marry him; I'm leaving you and Anglon forever." She slammed the door shut and padlocked it.

Hermas roared from within, "Let me out!"

Petrella swam out of the tower as fast as she could. It had worked—her fake illness. In fact, she felt stronger than usual. An exotic flower happened to slink in through the porthole with the seaweed and she ate it, realizing later it was a *Tarafoe*, the same petals the water warriors ate when they went to war. The petals were orange and they tasted bitter, but they provided endurance and strength when fighting.

Petrella charged through the water. Suddenly, the Anglon Kingdom's Palace bells chimed five times—a signal to round up the warriors. They would be coming after her; she swam faster.

Petrella arrived at Metalicah Pointe; her heart was racing. It was dusk. She checked the pier looking for

Finerd; he wasn't there. She swam closer to the RavenZedd Compound beach; her fin touched the sandy bottom as her eyes scanned the perimeter. But, the young man was nowhere to be found. There were a few humans on the beach, but none seemed to pay much attention to her because it was hard to see her head in the water with night approaching.

How will I get to Finerd? She needed his help to save her from Batavia and her tyrant father. Her only choice was to swim ashore, get out of the water, and ask a human for assistance. *I will have to risk getting caught and being thrown back into the sea, but what else can I do?*

She drew a breath and floated up on the sand. A few humans screeched, and some fled. After all, she was a Gillian. Someone called for help and two human males in dark blue clothing, guards of the compound, marched toward the beach, carrying *Zionic* guns—small handheld devices which emitted pulsing beams of light. If struck, the gun's electric current could be fatal.

The older male with fire-colored hair asked, "What are you doing here? You must leave immediately." He tried nudging her into the water.

In the distance, the guard saw hundreds of *Zioppa* rebels coming up from the water; his jaw dropped.

The younger male drew his weapon, "What the—"

Batavia appeared on the frontline with a bow and flaming arrow in his hand. He shouted, "She is one of ours. Give her back to us and we will leave in peace."

Frightened, Petrella lifted her head, grabbing onto the older guard. "Don't listen to him. They're rebels; you have no idea what they will do to me if you throw me back in the water."

The older guard knelt down beside her, "But we are not supposed to—"

"I know," she pleaded, "I came here to find Finerd. Can you help me find him, please?"

The younger guard shrugged, "I don't know who he is."

"I don't have much time. He works here. I will die if you put me in the water, or I will die here. I can only be on land for three hours. I need to see Finerd right away."

Batavia and his rebels pointed their bows and fiery arrows toward the compound guards and Petrella. "She has disobeyed the covenant by seeking relations with a Human. She will be tried in our court."

The older guard had a radio strapped to his shoulder. He called the compound, asking for Finerd and more backup. After a minute, a voice said Finerd had gone home.

Sirens rang out in the distance. The older guard looked down at Petrella. "My apologies but your friend is not here. This is not our problem. You are putting Humans in danger."

Tears streaked her cheeks. She wanted desperately to see Finerd one last time. "Please," she whimpered, "get him for me."

The older guard, smitten by Petrella's beauty and her circumstances, radioed the compound again. "Is there any way to get Finerd back here?"

"Hold on," came the voice on the other end.

His radio beeped. "We can send someone to find him. It might take a couple of hours."

The older guard gazed at Petrella. "Is that enough time?"

Petrella shook her head, "No, but just get him anyway, as soon as you can."

Giving instructions to the compound, both guards helped Petrella sit up on the sand. The younger one said, "What are we doing? She can't stay like this. Let's move her inside the compound and fill one of the tubs with water."

"No, don't move me," she begged.

The older one agreed and reached for one of her arms. "Okay, ready?"

Petrella screeched. "Please…Stop."

The younger guard replied, "But you'll die out here!"

She wrestled loose from their grip and slumped on the sand. Petrella was at a crossroad; either way, she would be dead soon. What were the odds that Finerd would get to her at all? Her energy depleted, she whispered, "Who am I fooling?"

The guards sat her up again. Without warning, a blazing arrow came through the air and struck the younger guard down.

Petrella screamed.

Batavia's voice boomed. "Move her near the water now, or you'll be next," he pointed to the older guard.

The older guard dropped Petrella on the beach. He started to run, but another flaming arrow flew through the air and struck and killed him.

Petrella yelled, "Away with your black heart, Batavia!"

Batavia started swimming toward her. "I'm coming to get you."

Petrella turned over on her back and looked up at the

blackening sky. The air felt heavy; she was parched, and her gills were beginning to chap.

Turning her head slowly toward the water, she saw Batavia getting closer. She sobbed. *I will never know love. I'm so sorry, Finerd.*

Petrella let her hands caress the sand until her left hand touched something cold and hard. She turned toward it. It was a knife, probably dropped there by one of the guards. She grabbed it.

A second later, Batavia had slid onto the sand and was on top of her body. "Here you are," he said, panting.

Petrella turned her head from side to side, not wanting to look in the evil man's face. *I will never be with him. Never!*

Grabbing her right arm, he pressed it into the sand and said, "You're mine!"

Her heart was weakening. Her lips were blistering. Petrella inhaled and with all her strength she lifted up her other arm, the one with the knife, and thrust it toward

Batavia's abdomen.

He lunged for the knife; it was inches from his flesh.

"Oh, no you don't."

They tugged at the weapon, but Petrella couldn't hold onto the knife much longer. She was fading fast. She glimpsed over at groups of human soldiers armed with Zionic guns, standing on the roof of the compound.

Suddenly, King Hermas and his Anglon warriors swam up to the surface. "Batavia, leave my daughter alone, expect fatal retribution if you do not obey my command!"

Batavia turned and howled back, while pushing the knife down toward Petrella. "…Never, old fool, you will not ruin my plans!"

War on Sand and in Water.

Flaming arrows swiftly crisscrossed the skies above Petrella. An arrow sank deep into Batavia's skull. His eyes rolled up in his head as he dropped down on top of her; the knife he still held tore into her gut.

Groaning weakly, Petrella exhaled her last breath.

King Hermas swam up on the sand. He pushed Batavia out of the way and seized his daughter by the arms. Shaking her, he bawled, "Come back to me!"

But it was too late, Petrella was dead.

At the sound of running feet, Hermas took the knife out of his daughter's flesh. "I have nothing now, my family is gone. They can take my kingdom and everything in it. It is over," he whispered, as he stabbed himself in the heart.

FINERD RACED TO THE SCENE and upon seeing all the bloodshed, he stumbled and fell. Batavia lay face down with an arrow in his head, Hermas lay with a knife sticking out of his chest, and Petrella's blood was pooling into the sand. He gagged.

Wiping his mouth, Finerd took Petrella in his arms, cradling her head to his chest, just above his star-shaped tattoo. "I was there at our pier every night, I waited for you. I...I fell in love with you. Oh, how I wish we could be together."

With tears in his eyes, he bent forward and gently kissed her dried lips. All of a sudden, the skies opened up and a shower of stars danced down upon them, like snowflakes.

Finerd looked up and around, surprised at the display taking place right before him. He laid Petrella down on the sand. Watching over her, he saw her stomach wound close up, and her fin turn into human legs.

He staggered backwards, amazed, "It can't be."

Petrella coughed and spit up. Her eyes opened and she recognized Finerd. "You're here?"

Finerd's body jerked forward with emotion, "...My sweet, sweet Petrella."

She smiled, letting the stars fall and tickle her face. "Look at what you've done," she stared upward. "It's a shower of stars."

He scratched his head. "I don't understand. It's like magic."

"No, it's not magic. It is real love. God's **Fifth Rule**— *Love each other always.*"

Trumpets sounded from the sky as a ray of light came through the clouds and shined upon them.

God's voice boomed from the Heavens. "You have pleased Me, Princess Petrella. You stayed true to yourself and steered away from the evils consuming the seas of Yemell."

Petrella squinted into the light remembering all the wisdom her mother had shared with her.

Trumpets sounded a second time.

"I have also witnessed your declaration of love for one another. And, that pleases Me very much."

Petrella leaned toward Finerd who had knelt down beside her. "Oh, Finerd…In a world full of chaos, I *now* believe with all my heart that true love can exist, just like the love Queen Bethsheeba felt for Medith."

A tear fell down Finerd's cheek. "Well, my dear Princess, you will have to tell me about Bethsheeba and Medith someday."

Trumpets sounded a third time.

God spoke once more. "You have My blessing. Go

forth. Live by My *Rules* and share them with others."

The young woman smiled toward the sky. "You have my word, Lord. We will do right for the prosperity of Yemell.

Carefully, Finerd lifted Petrella up onto her feet. Taking her hand in his, they walked into the moonlight and lived happily ever after.

Finerd and Princess Petrella, Together.

THE END

Increasing Your Vocabulary

Reading is such a rich experience. Sometimes, you might come across words that you aren't familiar with, or know their definition. Below, I compiled a short list of words you can look up in a dictionary.

Apathy	Relished
Perilous	Heeded
Fleeting	Defiance
Greed	Retaliation
Idolatry	Alliance
Militia	Wafting
Degenerates	Gallivanting
Tidal Island	Meticulous
Compound	Covenant
Betrothal	Dire Straits
Grapple	Cowered
Animosity	Waning

Study/Follow-Up Questions

1. What are God's *Five Rules* and why does He instill them? What do those rules mean to you?

2. How would you describe the Gillian species?

3. What religious book can the *Volumb* be compared to?

4. What does God want most from the Humans and Gillians?

5. What are some underlying themes in the book?

6. What does Petrella want most out of a romantic relationship?

7. Petrella goes against her father's mandate. How could her situation be handled differently?

8. What is the root of King Hermas' fury?

9. What is morally wrong with Bethsheeba and Medith's relationship? What is right about it?

10. Why is the *Zioppa* militia overthrowing kingdoms?

11. What is Batavia's goal after he marries Petrella?

12. What does Queen Azel represent to Petrella? Why did she tell all those stories to her daughter?

13. What is the meaning of Finerd's star tattoo?

14. How are President Tuskana and King Hermas alike?

15. What would happen if Humans and Gillians are found together?

16. What's an *Arowdithe*?

17. What is a *Tarafoe*?

18. What emits from a *Zionic* gun?

19. What is the moral of this story?

20. Write the next scene of the story. What will happen to Petrella and Finerd on Yemell?

To the Aspiring Writers and Illustrators

It's been said that writing and drawing are an introvert's endeavor. It's a quiet type of work from our thoughts, where words and pictures are formed.

Some days, the mind can be thriving with such emotion that creativity cannot come out fast enough. Other times, it's a blank page that stares back at you.

With strewn pages and assorted colored inks, one writes and draws from their innermost desires, hoping someone would find their writing and artwork worthwhile.

But regardless, don't write or draw to please others. But rather, do it for yourselves. Pursue the dream and make it *your* reality.

If it's in *you,* then you can *channel* it out of you.

72

Sketching with your Imagination

Creative artwork comes in all shapes and sizes. Grab a few crayons and markers and color in the pictures on the next few pages. You too can be an artist. Enjoy!

Princess Petrella

Princess Petrella

Princess Petrella

Petrella swimming

King Hermas

Prince Batavia

Prince Batavia

Petrella and Finerd at Metalicah Pointe

Dear Reader...

If you've enjoyed reading *Petrella, the Gillian Princess*, I would love it if you would help others enjoy this book, too. Here are some ways you can help spread the word:

Recommend it. Help other readers find this book by recommending it to friends, writing groups, reading groups, book clubs, and discussion forums.

Share it. Let other readers know you've read the book by posting a note on your social media pages and/or your *Goodreads* site.

Review it. Very important. Good, bad, or ugly, please tell others about this book. Review it on your favorite book site: *Amazon, Barnes and Noble*, and/or *Goodreads*.

Your support is greatly appreciated.

Other Books by the Author

Chiara Talluto's first novel, *Love's Perfect Surrender*, is a "grown-up" Christian Romance about a troubled married couple with flawed expectations and an imperfect, beautiful child who teaches them to surrender their expectations in order to mend their broken union. It's available via *Amazon* and *Barnes and Noble*.

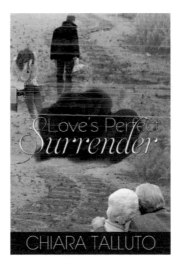

About the Author

Chicago-born, a full-time mother and author, Chiara Talluto, is known as the *Master Storyteller* in her household. She has a passion for writing about people who struggle with decisions and conflicts that arise in their lives.

Enchanted and inspired by many of Disney's fairy tales, this is her *very* first middle-grade short story.

Chiara hopes that this story will touch your heart so that you may see how meaningful true love can be. Petrella followed her heart, she was determined to succeed. Her determination helped her to make her dream become a reality. Chiara urges you to do the same.

Currently, Chiara is hard at work on her second novel, as well as penning other short stories. When she's not writing, she is either reading or playing mommy with her two young daughters. Her motto is: *Live, laugh and cry.*

More on Chiara, go to: www.chiaratalluto.com.

Acknowledgements

This short story was written in the fall of 2012 with the intention of it being part of an anthology. It never made the cut. Placed in a drawer, it sat patiently, waiting. I didn't find it until the fall of 2014 while rummaging through old paperwork.

After rereading it several times to myself and then to my daughters, I decided to bring the magic and imagination of *Petrella, the Gillian Princess* back to life. I spent the better part of 2015 and 2016 enhancing and streamlining the story to make it what it is today, a little gem for your enjoyment.

I thank God, who continually urges me to stick with this labor of writing as I spend hours upon hours wondering if the stories in my head will ever turn into something. No matter the wait, I've surrendered myself to carry on and pray for the right doors to open for me.

To my beautiful daughters, Ava and Stella. Every day,

you challenge me to take a risk, to write something that goes beyond my comfort zone, and follow my heart by telling honest and compelling stories. This is for you, my darlings. And, their sketches are for *you* to enjoy.

To my beta-readers: Hallie Koontz, Lisa Anders, Gabriella Biancofiore, and Marie Pupillo-Strauch. And, to my "Launch Team" readers. Thank you *all* for your attentiveness and feedback. I got it right because of you.

To my good friend, Lou Centrella, from our *Schaumburg Scribes* writers group; thank you for a wonderful cover design. I appreciate your friendship all these years. www.loucentrella.com.

To my editor and friend, Dennis De Rose, thank you for your smart insightful feedback. Petrella soars because of you.

To my husband, Joe, thank you for always being so supportive and loving in my pursuit of that special story because they are all *my* special stories.